Fact Finders™

Great Hispanics

Sammy Sosa

Baseball Superstar

by Nick Healy

Consultant:
Jim Gates
Library Director
National Baseball Hall of Fame and Museum
Cooperstown, New York

Capstone
press

Mankato, Minnesota

Fact Finders is published by Capstone Press,
151 Good Counsel Drive, P.O. Box 669, Mankato, Minnesota 56002.
www.capstonepress.com

Library of Congress Cataloging-in-Publication Data
Healy, Nick.
    Sammy Sosa: baseball superstar / by Nick Healy.
    p. cm. — (Fact finders. Biographies. Great Hispanics)
    Summary: "An introduction to the life of Sammy Sosa, the Hispanic man who was born in
the Dominican Republic and became a baseball superstar, while still remembering and giving
to his home country and family"—Provided by publisher.
    Includes bibliographical references and index.
    ISBN-13: 978-0-7368-5443-6 (hardcover)
    ISBN-10: 0-7368-5443-6 (hardcover)
    1. Sosa, Sammy, 1968—Juvenile literature. 2. Baseball players—Dominican Republic—
Biography—Juvenile literature. I. Title. II. Series.
GV865.S59H43 2006
796.357'092—dc22   2005021592

Editorial Credits
Amber Bannerman, editor; Juliette Peters, set designer; Linda Clavel and Scott Thoms,
    designers; Wanda Winch, photo researcher/photo editor

Photo Credits
AP Photo/Beth A. Keiser, 22; Michael S. Green, 18
The Baltimore Sun/Elizabeth Malby, 26
Corbis/Reinhard Eisele, 8–9
Getty Images Inc./AFP/Daniel Lippitt, 20–21; AFP/John Zich, 5, 6, 23; AFP/Stephen Jaffe, 7;
    Jonathan Daniel, 15, 19; MLB photos/Doug Dukane, cover; MLB photos/Jeff Carlick, 17;
    Ronald Martinez, 1, 13
Globe Photo Inc., 11
Image Courtesy of Mark Nickerson, 14
SportsChrome, Inc./Rob Tringali, 25, 27

1 2 3 4 5 6 11 10 09 08 07 06

Table of Contents

Chapter 1

Home Run Chase

On September 13, 1998, Chicago Cubs star right fielder, Sammy Sosa, gripped his bat. It was the ninth **inning**, and the Cubs were battling the Milwaukee Brewers. Sosa had already hit a home run in the fifth inning. If he smashed another one, he would tie the current home run record of 62 in a single season.

When the pitch came, Sosa took a powerful swing. The ball soared toward the left field wall. Sosa touched two fingers to his mouth and blew a kiss. Then he said, *"Para ti Mami,"* which means, "For you, Mommy," as he hopped, then trotted toward first base.

Sosa is carried off the field by his teammates after hitting his 62nd home run on September 13, 1998.

The game paused for six minutes while fans cheered at Chicago's Wrigley Field. In the Dominican Republic, where Sosa grew up, people celebrated in the streets. Sosa had just hit his 62nd home run of the season.

Sixty-Two

All summer, the number 62 had been on the minds of baseball fans around the world. The previous single season record was 61 home runs. Sosa and St. Louis Cardinal Mark McGwire spent the 1998 season chasing the record. As it turned out, McGwire was the first to reach the record mark on September 8.

A fan keeps track of Sosa's 62nd home run with a sign.

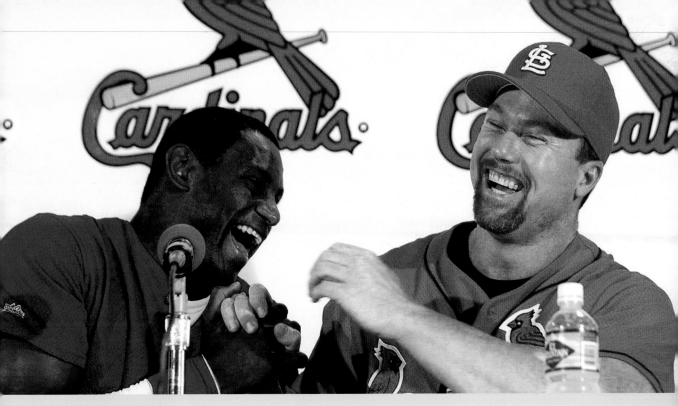

QUOTE

"I feel great to be
there with Babe Ruth,
Roger Maris, and
Mark McGwire."
—Sammy Sosa

When Sosa hit his 62nd home run, the two were tied again. Nobody knew who would finish the season with the new record.

Even though Sosa and McGwire were competitors, they were still friends. They supported, encouraged, and looked up to each other throughout their chase for the home run record.

Chapter 2

Early Life

Samuel Peralta Sosa was born November 12, 1968, in San Pedro de Macorís, Dominican Republic. He was the fifth of six children in his family. He was very close to his family. When Sosa was 7, his father, Juan, died.

Sosa's mother, Lucrecia, sold meals to factory workers to earn money for her family. Her children also worked. After school, Sosa shined shoes and washed cars. He gave the money to his mother.

Sosa started going to school less and working more. He dropped out of school when he was in eighth grade. He worked to earn money for his family instead.

San Pedro de Macorís is Sosa's hometown.

Boxing to Baseball

When Sosa was young,
he didn't dream of becoming
a baseball player. Instead,
he wanted to be a boxer.
His mother disapproved of
this. She didn't want her son
to get hurt. His brother, Luis,
introduced him to baseball.

When Sosa wasn't
working, he'd play baseball
on the street with friends.
They used wadded tape for
a ball and a stick for a bat.
Their gloves were old milk
cartons cut in half.

Sosa saw baseball players from all over the world become rich and famous. He wanted to be like them. Sosa especially admired famous Puerto Rican baseball player Roberto Clemente.

Sosa worked hard. It was important to him to be good at what he did. He woke up early every morning to exercise and practice baseball.

Roberto Clemente smacks one of his 3,000 hits. ▼

Chapter 3

A Young Pro

When Sosa was 17, Omar Minaya, a **major league** baseball **scout**, invited Sosa to a tryout in Puerto Plata, Dominican Republic. Tall, scrawny Sosa rode a bus for four hours to reach the city. He showed up at the field in a borrowed uniform. His shoes had holes in them.

Minaya worked for the Texas Rangers. He could see past Sosa's appearance. And he could see a spark in Sosa that he didn't see in other players. He saw not only a hitter with a good swing, but also a hard worker.

General Manager Omar Minaya (left), of the New York Mets, visits with General Manager John Schuerholz (right), of the Atlanta Braves.

Minaya went to the Sosa family's tiny two-room home. He offered Sosa $3,500 to sign with the Rangers. The teenager took the deal. He gave most of the money to his mother.

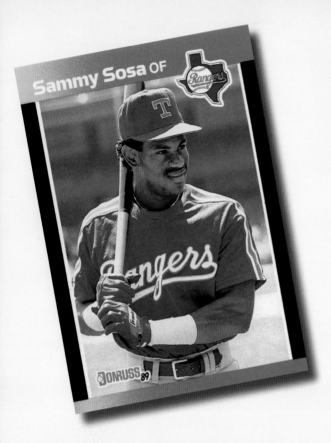

Sosa's 1989 rookie baseball card shows him playing for the Texas Rangers.

Climbing to the Majors

In spring 1986, Sosa took a flight from the Dominican Republic to the United States. He knew only a few words of English. He joined the Rangers' **minor league** team in Sarasota, Florida.

In pro baseball, most players start in the minor leagues. They work on improving their skills. If they play well, they sometimes get called up to play in the major leagues.

In June 1989, the Rangers offered Sosa a major league position. After a good start, Sosa skidded to a very low batting average. The Rangers sent him back to the minors. Then they traded Sosa to the Chicago White Sox.

By the end of the season, Sosa was back in the major leagues. However, his struggles at the plate continued. Being a superstar seemed a long way off.

Sosa slides toward first base. ▼

Chapter 4

A Slugging Star

Sosa was called a free swinger. He often swung at pitches out of the strike zone. He struck out a lot. Some said he was a selfish player. They said he was more worried about his own **statistics** than his team's success. But others believed Sosa's problem was his age. He was only 24 years old, and he was still learning.

In 1992, the White Sox gave up on Sosa. They traded him across town to the Chicago Cubs.

Sosa connects with a pitch during a game at Candlestick Park in San Francisco, California.

▲ Sammy and Sonia kiss during "Sammy Sosa Day" at Wrigley Field.

FACT!

Sosa chose Roberto Clemente's number, 21. Clemente was the first Latino baseball player voted into the Hall of Fame.

Marriage and Family

Sosa's personal life also changed during the months between the 1991 and 1992 baseball seasons. After the season ended in 1991, Sosa married Sonia Rodríguez. Sonia was also a Dominican.

Sosa and his wife had four children over several years. For many years, the whole family lived in Chicago during the baseball season. They would return to the Dominican Republic for the winter.

Breakthrough

In 1992, injuries shortened Sosa's first season with the Cubs. But he took a huge step forward the next year. Sosa became the first Cubs player to top 30 home runs and 30 stolen bases in the same season.

That year began a string of quality seasons. In 1994, Sosa had a .300 batting average for the first time. He played in his first All-Star game in 1995.

Sosa's abilities won him **fame**. In 1997, the Cubs gave Sosa a four-year contract for $42.5 million. Only two other major league players were paid more.

Sosa throws a ball in from the outfield during a game against the Kansas City Royals. ▼

19

The Record Race

The 1998 home run battle between Sosa and Mark McGwire thrilled fans everywhere. **Journalists** and TV crews followed the two closely as summer moved into fall.

Excitement was in the air. Fans cheered Sosa on, hoping he'd keep smacking the ball. Crowds stood and applauded when he stepped up to bat.

Sosa did it all that year. He had a high batting average and had many home runs. He also led the Cubs into the play-offs. They had not made the play-offs in nearly 10 years.

In the end, Sosa lost the home run record. McGwire finished with 70, while Sosa had 66.

SAMMY: C

U'RE THE MAN

Sosa runs a lap around Wrigley Field as fans cheer him on before a game against the Cincinnati Reds.

▲ A sign at Wrigley Field congratulates Sammy Sosa just after he was named MVP.

Most Valuable Player

Despite McGwire's record, many sportswriters believed Sosa had a better year. After the season, the writers voted Sosa the Most Valuable Player (MVP) of the National League.

The next few years were nearly as good for Sosa. He became the only player to have three seasons with 60 or more home runs.

QUOTE

"When they mention Mark McGwire, they will mention me. Fifty years from now, I hope that they remember me, too. After all, I was there with him."

—Sammy Sosa

Fans continued flocking to Chicago's Wrigley Field to see Sosa. They liked the way he played. They loved his full-speed dash to right field at the game's start. They liked his springy hop at home plate after smacking a long ball. They also loved watching his home runs clear the ivy-covered walls.

Sosa does his famous hop after hitting a home run. ➤

Chapter 6

Giving His All

For years, Sosa remained a popular player as a member of the Cubs. He was known for his wide smile and his wicked swing. And he continued to belt home runs and drive in runs.

However, Sosa's time with the Cubs ended after 13 seasons. Just before the 2005 season, the Cubs traded Sosa to the Baltimore Orioles. At the time, he was seventh on the all-time list for career home runs. He was 36 years old and just 26 home runs short of 600. Only four players in major league history have topped that mark.

Sosa now plays for the Baltimore Orioles.

▲ A statue of Sosa stands outside a mall Sosa donated money to in San Pedro de Macorís.

QUOTE

"I'd rather people remember me for being a good person first and a good player second."
—Sammy Sosa

Remembering Others

Sosa uses his wealth and fame to help people back home. He's bought computers for Dominican schools. When a hurricane hit his island, he sent emergency supplies for people without food and shelter. He also built a baseball school for young players. In December, Sosa sometimes acts as "Sammy Claus" and provides gifts for poor children.

Today, Sosa is a baseball superstar. Long after he hangs up his glove, fans will remember his record-breaking bat and his home run hop. People will also remember his kind heart.

Fast Facts

Full name: Samuel Peralta Sosa
Birth: November 12, 1968
Hometown: San Pedro de Macorís, Dominican Republic
Parents: Juan Bautista Montero and Lucrecia Sosa
Siblings: Three brothers and two sisters
Wife: Sonia
Children: Keysha, Kenia, Sammy Jr., and Michael
Career stats through 2005:
    Hits: 2,304
    Games: 2,240
    Home runs: 588
    Runs batted in (RBIs): 1,575
    Batting average: .274
All-Star games: 1995, 1998–2002, 2004
National League MVP: 1998
Roberto Clemente Award: 1998

Time Line

Sammy Sosa is born in San Pedro de Macorís, Dominican Republic.

Sosa plays in his first major league game for the Texas Rangers. Later that year, the Rangers trade him to the Chicago White Sox.

Sosa signs his first professional contract.

Sosa marries Sonia Rodríguez.

1968   **1985**   **1989**   **1991**

1972   **1974**   **1986**   **1991**

Events in History

Puerto Rican baseball star Roberto Clemente dies in a plane crash.

The Challenger space shuttle explodes during launch.

United States President Richard Nixon resigns. Gerald Ford becomes president.

The Persian Gulf War is fought between Iraq and 39 other countries.

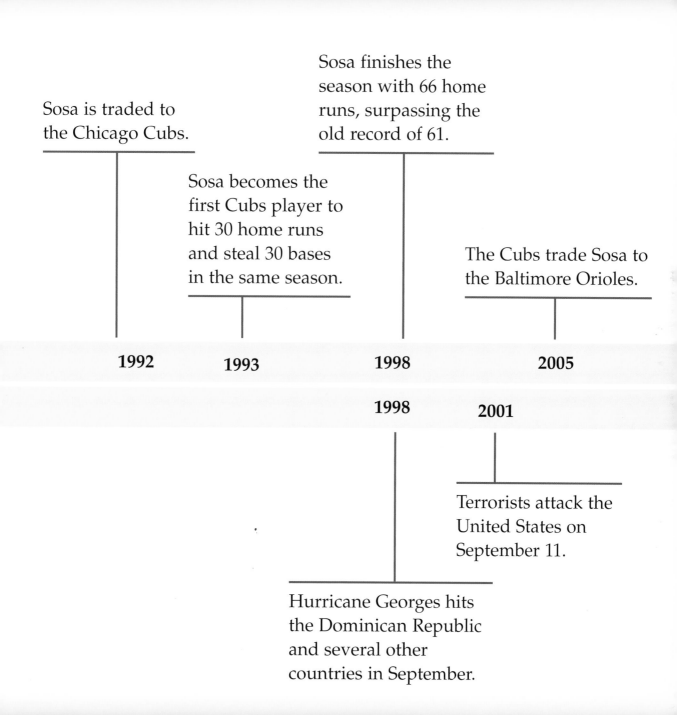

Sosa is traded to
the Chicago Cubs.

Sosa finishes the
season with 66 home
runs, surpassing the
old record of 61.

Sosa becomes the
first Cubs player to
hit 30 home runs
and steal 30 bases
in the same season.

The Cubs trade Sosa to
the Baltimore Orioles.

1992   **1993**   **1998**   **2005**

1998   **2001**

Terrorists attack the
United States on
September 11.

Hurricane Georges hits
the Dominican Republic
and several other
countries in September.

Glossary

fame (FAYM)—being well known

inning (IN-ing)—a part of a baseball game in which each team gets a turn at bat

journalist (JUR-nuhl-ist)—someone who collects information and writes articles for newspapers, magazines, TV, or radio

major league (MAY-jur LEEG)—the highest playing level of professional baseball

minor league (MYE-nur LEEG)—a professional level of baseball under major league

scout (SKOUT)—a person whose job is to discover talented ballplayers

statistic (stuh-TISS-tik)—a fact shown as a number or percentage

Internet Sites

FactHound offers a safe, fun way to find Internet sites related to this book. All of the sites on FactHound have been researched by our staff.

Here's how:

1. Visit *www.facthound.com*
2. Type in this special code: **0736854436** for age-appropriate sites. Or enter a search word related to this book for a more general search.
3. Click on the **Fetch It** button.

FactHound will fetch the best sites for you!

Read More

Savage, Jeff. *Sammy Sosa.* Amazing Athletes. Minneapolis: LernerSports, 2005.

Silverstone, Michael. *Latino Legends: Hispanics in Major League Baseball.* High Five Reading. Bloomington, Minn.: Red Brick Learning, 2004.

Torres, John Albert. *Sports Great Sammy Sosa.* Sports Great Books. Berkeley Heights, N.J.: Enslow Publishers, 2003.

Index